Is There Room on the Feather Bed?

by
Libba Moore Gray

illustrated by
Nadine Bernard Westcott

ORCHARD BOOKS
NEW YORK

For Lynne Harrison
  —L.M.G.

For Becky
  —N.B.W.

Text copyright © 1997 by The Estate of Elizabeth M. Gray
Illustrations copyright © 1997 by Nadine Bernard Westcott
First Orchard Paperbacks edition 1999

Orchard Books, A Grolier Company
95 Madison Avenue, New York, NY 10016

Manufactured in China
Printed by Toppan Printing Company, Inc.
Book design by Sylvia Frezzolini Severance

Hardcover 10 9 8 7 6 5 4 3 2
Paperback 10 9 8 7 6 5 4 3 2 1

The text of this book is set in 14 point Sabon.
The illustrations are black ink line and watercolor.

Library of Congress Cataloging-in-Publication Data
Gray, Libba Moore.
   Is there room on the feather bed? / by Libba Moore Gray ;
illustrated by Nadine Bernard Westcott.
      p. cm. "A Melanie Kroupa book"—Half t.p.
   Summary: One rainy night a wee fat man and his wee fat wife are joined
in their feather bed by a variety of animals including a skunk.
ISBN 0-531-30013-7 (tr.) ISBN 0-531-33013-3 (lib. bdg.) ISBN 0-531-07137-5 (pbk.)
[1. Domestic animals—Fiction. 2. Skunks—Fiction.]
I. Westcott, Nadine Bernard, ill. II. Title.
PZ7.G7793Is   1997   [E]—dc20   96-42387

Once there was a wee fat man and a wee fat woman
who lived in a teeny tiny house at the bottom of a great green hill
next to the bank of a clear running brook.

They lived happily there with a large family of animals.

There was a green-headed goose, a yellow-billed duck, a woolly white sheep, a speckled black hen, a fat pink pig, a furry brown dog, an orange-spotted cow, and a grinning gray cat.

And from time to time a small plump skunk with a broad white stripe down the center of its bushy back stood upwind watching them. The other animals never let him get too close: they ran away whenever he came near.

When the wind blew on the teeny tiny house at the bottom of the great green hill, it blew hard. And when the sun shone, it shone brightly.

One day the wind blew a dark cloud across the brightly shining sun. Soon the rain started with a quiet *ping ping ping*. Before long the pinging turned into the loud hammering of a thousand drops that ran off the red tile roof, splashed into the rain barrel, and trickled down the bank of the clear running brook.

The brook overflowed its banks and rose so high that the green-headed goose and the yellow-billed duck could no longer enjoy a good swim. So they waddled up the bank and stood under a willow tree.

That night the wee fat man and the wee fat woman were getting ready for a good night's sleep when there came a tapping on their door.

The wee fat woman opened it.

"*Honk honk honk,*
Quack quack quack,
the rain is pouring
on our feathered backs,"

said the green-headed goose and the yellow-billed duck.

"*Why, bless your hearts,*
such a noise, such a fuss.
There's room on the feather bed
for all of us,"

said the wee fat woman.

So the wee fat man and the wee fat woman made room for the goose and the duck, and they all settled in for a good night's sleep.

No sooner had their eyes closed than there came a second
tapping on the door. The wee fat woman opened it. There stood
the woolly white sheep and the speckled black hen, who said,

"*Baa baa baa,*
Cluck cluck cluck,
may we please join
the goose and the duck?"

"*Why, bless your hearts,*
such a noise, such a fuss.
There's room on the feather bed
for all of us,"

answered the wee fat woman.

And so the wee fat man and
the wee fat woman and the goose
and the duck and the sheep and the hen
all curled up on the feather bed
and closed their eyes.

Soon there was more tapping on the door. Outside stood
the fat pink pig and the furry brown dog, who said,

"*Oink oink oink,*
Woof woof woof,
may we stay beneath
your warm dry roof?"

And the wee fat woman welcomed them too.

"*Why, bless your hearts,*
such a noise, such a fuss.
There's room on the feather bed
for all of us."

So they all moved over, and soon the
wee fat man and the wee fat woman and the
goose and the duck and the sheep and the
hen and the pig and the dog were sound asleep.

Just as a nice dream was beginning for them all, there came another tap on the door. The wee fat woman opened it, and this time the orange-spotted cow and the grinning gray cat stood outside in a large puddle of water. They said,

"*Meow meow meow,*
Moo moo moo,
we'd like to come in
till the sky turns blue."

The wee fat woman welcomed them kindly as well,
and a place was made for them on the feather bed, which
by now was a little crowded.

Soon they were all fast asleep.

Outside, the water was rising higher and higher, and rising right along with it was the teeny tiny house. It rocked gently as if it were a cradle—helping everyone to sleep soundly indeed.

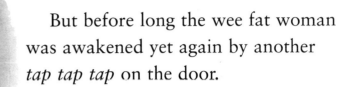

But before long the wee fat woman was awakened yet again by another *tap tap tap* on the door.

TAP
TAP
TAP

A now very sleepy wee fat woman opened it and was astonished to find the small plump skunk, who sang out,

"*I'm a small plump skunk
who cannot swim.
I'm asking politely,
may I please come in?*"

The wee fat woman scooped up the small skunk and said,

"*Why, bless your heart,
such a noise, such a fuss.
There's room on the feather bed
for all of us.*"

SKUNK!!

But when she helped him up onto the bed,
the green-headed goose woke up and cried . . .

And with that,
the wee fat man, the green-headed goose
and the yellow-billed duck, the woolly white sheep
and the speckled black hen, the fat pink pig and
the furry brown dog, the orange-spotted cow
and the grinning gray cat scattered
into the dark wet night!

It didn't take long before they began to think about the soft dry feather bed.

Finally, the green-headed goose called out to the others,

"Maybe we shouldn't have raised such a fuss. Skunk's cozy inside—But just look at us!"

Inside, the wee fat woman and the
small plump skunk were beginning to worry
about the wee fat man and the other animals
when they heard a tapping at the door.
The wee fat woman opened it.

"Honk! Honk! Honk!
Achoo! Achoo!
We've been so silly—
Is there room for us too?"

said the green-headed goose.

"Why, bless your hearts,
such a noise, such a fuss.
There's room on the feather bed
for all of us!

"So come back inside.
Let's all be friends.
We'll have breakfast in bed
until the rain ends,"

said the wee fat woman.

And so they did.